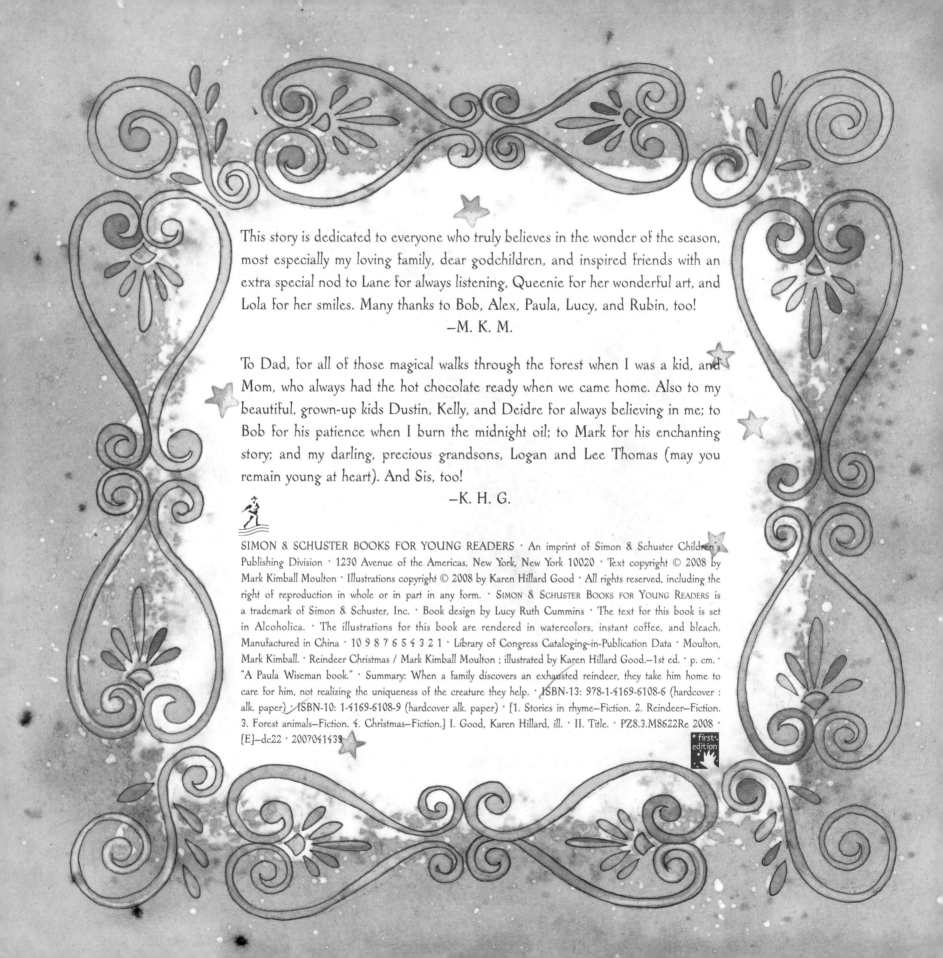

This story is dedicated to everyone who truly believes in the wonder of the season, most especially my loving family, dear godchildren, and inspired friends with an extra special nod to Lane for always listening, Queenie for her wonderful art, and Lola for her smiles. Many thanks to Bob, Alex, Paula, Lucy, and Rubin, too!

–M. K. M.

To Dad, for all of those magical walks through the forest when I was a kid, and Mom, who always had the hot chocolate ready when we came home. Also to my beautiful, grown-up kids Dustin, Kelly, and Deidre for always believing in me; to Bob for his patience when I burn the midnight oil; to Mark for his enchanting story; and my darling, precious grandsons, Logan and Lee Thomas (may you remain young at heart). And Sis, too!

–K. H. G.

SIMON & SCHUSTER BOOKS FOR YOUNG READERS · An imprint of Simon & Schuster Children's Publishing Division · 1230 Avenue of the Americas, New York, New York 10020 · Text copyright © 2008 by Mark Kimball Moulton · Illustrations copyright © 2008 by Karen Hillard Good · All rights reserved, including the right of reproduction in whole or in part in any form. · SIMON & SCHUSTER BOOKS FOR YOUNG READERS is a trademark of Simon & Schuster, Inc. · Book design by Lucy Ruth Cummins · The text for this book is set in Alcoholica. · The illustrations for this book are rendered in watercolors, instant coffee, and bleach. Manufactured in China · 10 9 8 7 6 5 4 3 2 1 · Library of Congress Cataloging-in-Publication Data · Moulton, Mark Kimball. · Reindeer Christmas / Mark Kimball Moulton ; illustrated by Karen Hillard Good.—1st ed. · p. cm. · "A Paula Wiseman book." · Summary: When a family discovers an exhausted reindeer, they take him home to care for him, not realizing the uniqueness of the creature they help. · ISBN-13: 978-1-4169-6108-6 (hardcover : alk. paper) · ISBN-10: 1-4169-6108-9 (hardcover alk. paper) · [1. Stories in rhyme—Fiction. 2. Reindeer—Fiction. 3. Forest animals—Fiction. 4. Christmas—Fiction.] I. Good, Karen Hillard, ill. · II. Title. · PZ8.3.M8622Re 2008 · [E]—dc22 · 2007041433

Reindeer Christmas

written by
MARK Kimball moulton

illustrated by
Karen Hillard Good

A Paula Wiseman Book
Simon & Schuster Books for Young Readers
New York   London   Toronto   Sydney

A December snow is falling, lightly dusting all the trees,
blanketing the forest in a crystal filigree.

The basket that I carry holds a tasty late-night treat—
carrots, corn, and apples for our forest friends to eat.

We sprinkle all the goodies on the pure-white, snow-capped ground,
then watch the thankful animals begin to gather 'round.

Deer and birds and bunnies come, and lots of playful mice;
we've even had a regal moose indulge us once or twice!

Each visit from our woodland friends makes us feel oh so blessed,
but there's one special visit that stands out above the rest. . . .

'Twas late one snowy evening—Christmas Day would be here soon,
when in the frosted forest something shimmered like the moon.

We saw the slightest movement and the flicker of an ear,
and suddenly we knew that what was glowing was a deer!

But as we watched, he stumbled and then fell into the snow.
He closed his eyes and soon began to lose his subtle glow.

He looked so cold and hungry as he shivered in the storm,
Grandma said, "Let's bring him in and make him toasty warm!"

We ran outside and touched the deer;
he opened just one eye,
and magically he seemed to float—
he almost seemed to fly!

We wrapped our arms around him
and we gently helped him in
and brought him to the fire,
where he floated down again.

He settled on a blanket; then Gram urged us,
"Let him be.
With food and warmth and rest,
he'll be good as new. You'll see."

She placed a bowl beside him
filled with apples, grain, and more.
He ate a bit, then closed his eyes
and soon began to snore.

Much later in the evening
        something woke me from my dreams;
my room was softly shimmering
        from luminescent beams.

I peered out of the window
        and could not believe my eyes.
I thought I saw our friend, the deer,
        fly straight across the sky.

I tiptoed to the fireplace to see if he was there,
but sure enough, our deer was gone—he wasn't anywhere.

The next day it was Christmas Eve
and we had much to do;
we found the perfect tree and then
we wrapped our presents too.

That night we all slept soundly
as we dreamed of Christmas morn,
when we would wake and celebrate
the day our Christ was born.

The sunrise had us leaping from our beds excitedly
and bounding barefoot down the stairs, shouting out in glee.

Grandma served us breakfast—then she smiled in pure delight
as we enjoyed each gift that Santa'd left for us that night.

And when we thought the gifts were done,
Gram reached beneath the tree
and handed a small wooden box
and Christmas card to me.

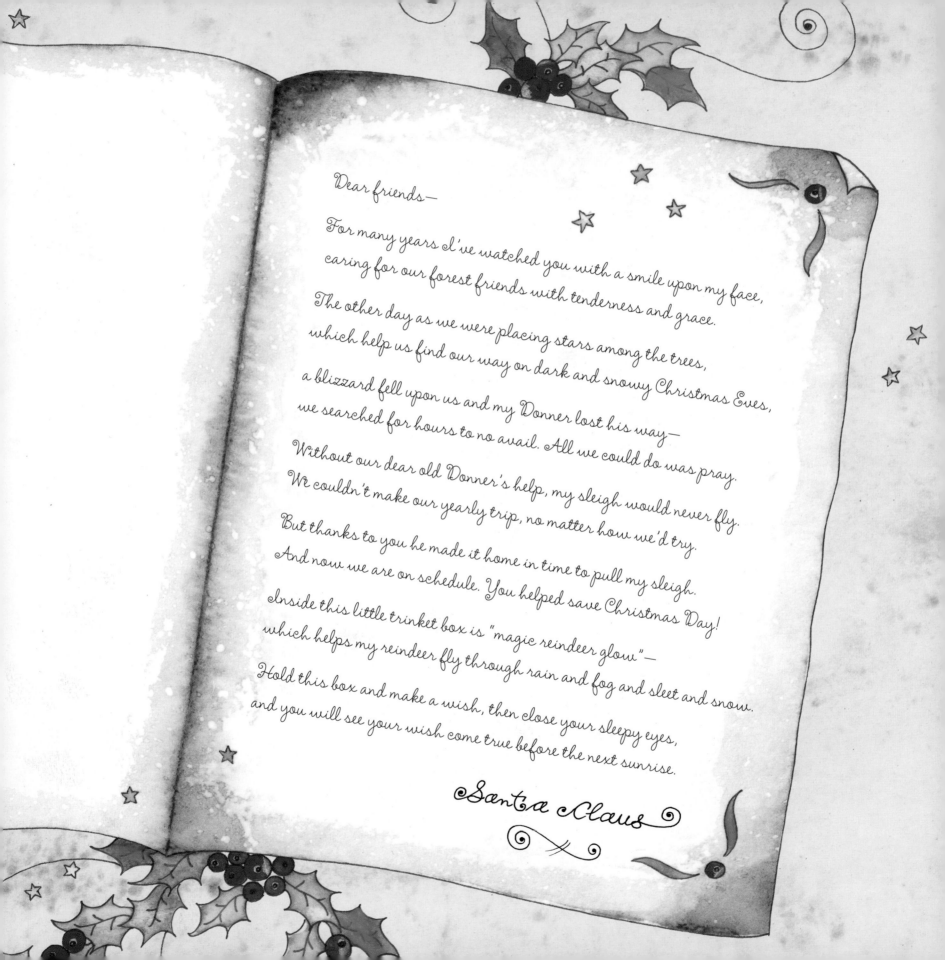

Dear friends—

For many years I've watched you with a smile upon my face,
caring for our forest friends with tenderness and grace.

The other day as we were placing stars among the trees,
which help us find our way on dark and snowy Christmas Eves,
a blizzard fell upon us and my Donner lost his way—
we searched for hours to no avail. All we could do was pray.

Without our dear old Donner's help, my sleigh would never fly.
We couldn't make our yearly trip, no matter how we'd try.

But thanks to you he made it home in time to pull my sleigh.
And now we are on schedule. You helped save Christmas Day!

Inside this little trinket box is "magic reindeer glow"—
which helps my reindeer fly through rain and fog and sleet and snow.

Hold this box and make a wish, then close your sleepy eyes,
and you will see your wish come true before the next sunrise.

Santa Claus

Our forest friends still visit us
each and every night,
and we still watch them
by the warm, soft glow of candlelight.

The wooden box that Santa left
was placed into my care.
I've treasured it for all these years,
as magic is so rare.

I've wanted the most perfect wish
that there could ever be,
and finally this special wish
has just occurred to me.

So now I'll close my eyes and hope
my heartfelt wish comes true . . .

I wish you
Peace
and Happiness
and Love
the whole year
through.

The End